500

A catalogue record for this book is available from the British Library

Adapted from the television script by Keith Littler, based on the original stories by Colin Reader.
Photographs by James Lampard.

Published by Ladybird Books Ltd.
80 Strand London WC2R 0RL
A Penguin Company

7 9 10 8

ISBN-13: 978-1-84422-483-8
ISBN-10: 1-8442-2483-X

Printed in China

Big Bang

It was a bright, sunny morning in Babblebrook. Stan and Little Red Tractor were at Top Acre Field.

Stan held out a half eaten stalk of corn.

"The birds have been at my crop again. I need something to scare them away!"

"Toot! Toot!" agreed Little Red Tractor.

Stan had an idea.

"Got it," he cried, jumping aboard Little Red Tractor. "Come on, back to Gosling Farm!"

Down the lane, they met Stumpy and Nipper. Nipper bobbed his lights to say hello to Little Red Tractor.

"I'm going to make a scarecrow," Stan explained to Stumpy. "Do you have any old clothes?"

"I'm sure Elsie can find a few!" Stumpy chuckled.

Little Red Tractor tooted goodbye as Nipper sped off.

On the lane back to the windmill, Nipper and Stumpy were suddenly scared by a huge BANG!

Stumpy shot up in his seat as Nipper swerved towards the ditch. "Whoa!" he cried in alarm.

Little Red Tractor and Stan were at Gosling Farm when...

BANG! Everyone jumped.

Patch ran into the barn and hid. "You all right, lad?" asked Stan.

"Those bangs must be frightening all the animals in the area," Stan complained. "Come on Little Red Tractor, let's go and investigate."

"Toot! Toot!" agreed Little Red Tractor, rolling his headlights as Stan jumped aboard.

At Beech garage, Walter and Nicola had heard the noises too. "I fell off my ladder and Nicola spilt oil on her overalls!" Walter explained to Stan.

Suddenly, they were all startled by another loud BANG!

"I wish they would stop," sighed Nicola. Stan decided to go and see Mr Jones. Perhaps he could shed some light on things.

"It's a gas driven bird scaring machine," explained Mr Jones, showing Stan a machine in his field. "Its loud bangs scare the birds away from my corn."

"It's scaring half the neighbourhood too!" said Stan.

"They'll get used to it in no time," laughed Mr Jones.

Stan told Mr Jones about his scarecrow idea, but Mr Jones just laughed.

"It's all about technology Stan," he said.

Stan, Amy and Ryan made the scarecrow.
"It needs clothes," announced Amy.
"Toot! Toot!" agreed Little Red Tractor.
"Stumpy's got some old clothes," said Stan.
"I bet that's him now!"
There was another loud BANG from Mr Jones' field. It caused Nipper to skid towards the barn.

"What IS that
infernal racket?"
huffed Stumpy.
Suddenly Stan had
another idea. He and
Little Red Tractor set off for
Beech Garage.

Stan told Nicola and Walter all about the gas driven bird scaring machine.

"So that's why he wants all these gas bottles," said Nicola.

Stan explained his plan to give Mr Jones empty gas bottles.

Then the bird scarer wouldn't work and perhaps Mr Jones would use something quieter in future! Everyone agreed it was a good plan and Nicola got to work.

The following morning Stan's field was quiet. AND there wasn't a bird in sight!

Amy and Ryan thought the scarecrow looked great.

"And there are no big bangs either," laughed Stan.

"Toot! Toot!" piped up Little Red Tractor happily.

Then they caught sight of Big Blue coming up the lane with Mr Jones. Chug, chug, chug!

"What are we going to tell him?" whispered Amy.

No one had thought about that!

Big Blue pulled up and Mr Jones leant out. "I see you have your scarecrow finished."

"He's working too," said Amy. "Look, no birds!"

Mr Jones, on the other hand, had a field full of birds and he had noticed a distinct lack of bangs that morning.

"Do you think my bird scarer has broken…?" he asked.

Stan stepped forward sheepishly. "Ah yes, you see…"

Mr Jones carried on…"I check the pipes; I check the control box…nothing wrong there. So I call the repairman and you'll never guess what he finds…"

"Er...empty gas bottles?" said Stan.

Ryan and Amy hid behind Little Red Tractor.

"Correct. Empty gas bottles. So I called the garage. Nicola told me the whole story."

"But you must agree your bird scarer was making a lot of noise," said Stan.

Mr Jones did agree.

"Perhaps your scarecrow experts might make one for me," smiled Mr Jones.

Amy and Ryan happily agreed.

"But if the birds come back, so does my machine," Mr Jones warned.

Big Blue honked goodbye and they chugged off.

Just then, there was a familiar revving and Nipper screeched to a halt.

"Seems a lot quieter today," chuckled Stumpy. "Now I can ride Nipper without those nasty bangs."

Vroom! Nipper revved up and away they went.

"Toot-Toot - BANG!" went Little Red Tractor, as he backfired his engine.

Nipper was so surprised that he shot into a ditch in panic.

"On no! Not again!" cried Stumpy.

"Little Red Tractor! Did you do that on purpose?" laughed Stan.

"Toot! Toot!" beeped Little Red Tractor, cheekily rolling his headlights!

500
500
500

500
500
500